oon Rock

Boriana and Vladimir Todorov   SIMPLY READ BOOKS

ELLIOT BADE WAS ALMOST OUT OF BREATH when he reached the burning house.

He had been running like mad, not sure what he would find. Now he knew. It was his house!

On fire!

He stood there for a moment, trying to take it all in. Then everything became a blur: the fire trucks, the ambulance, the group of neighbors gathered on the sidewalk. Elliot recognized some of the faces when they turned towards him. He could see their lips moving, but he could not make out what they were saying. It was almost as if someone had turned the sound off. All he could hear was his heart, thumping away in his chest. He dropped his bag on the ground, pushed through the crowd, and ran towards his home. He was almost there, when someone grabbed him from behind. The powerful hands of a firefighter picked him up and carried him away. Elliot began to kick and scream, trying to break free. "Let me go! Where's my mom? Is she okay?" he cried.

"She's been hurt, son," said the firefighter, pointing towards the ambulance. Elliot saw his mother being wheeled towards it on a stretcher. She was covered with blankets and wearing an oxygen mask. Her face was smudged with soot. Her eyes were closed. He tried to pull free again, but the firefighter held him tight. "You can't see her now. She needs to go to the hospital." The ambulance doors slammed shut, and with sirens blaring, it took off into the night. Elliot could do nothing but look on, his eyes filling up with tears.

Suddenly, a woman offered him a handkerchief. It was Mrs. Gibson, who lived around the corner and who used to work with his mother at the local library. She was holding something swaddled in a grey towel.

"Nobody saw how the fire started, Elliot," Mrs. Gibson began, as she carefully placed the little bundle in his hands. "Your mom managed to get out in time, but then she remembered Apollo… and went back in to fetch her." As if on cue, a cat's head emerged from inside the folds of the towel.

"Apollo!" Elliot cried out in relief, hugging the petrified creature to his chest. Apart from a few singed whiskers, Apollo seemed to be perfectly fine.

"You can stay with us tonight," said Mrs. Gibson, and then added, "Your granddad will pick you up tomorrow morning."

Elliot was not sure he had heard right. Granddad! What granddad? He did not have a grandfather. As far back as he could remember it had always been him, his mom, and good old Apollo. No one else, no relatives. Just them. Someone must have made a mistake! He would get up tomorrow and go to the hospital to help take care of his mom. She would need him to be there.

Elliot looked up at Mrs. Gibson. She tried to smile. "Let's go get some rest. Okay?"

He slowly turned away from the fire and followed her down the street.

· ● ·

By the time he got to Mrs. Gibson's house, Elliot was so tired that he went straight to bed with Apollo curled up at his feet. Next thing he knew, there was a gentle hand shaking him awake and the sound of an impatient car horn coming from outside.

"Time to go, Elliot. Your grandfather's waiting for you," Mrs. Gibson said lightly.

Elliot got up and rushed to the window. There on the street was an ancient-looking car, polished to a mirror finish. It was big and black, with a long hood and shiny chrome wheels and grille. By its side stood a very tall, elderly gentleman, dressed in a suit and tie. He glanced at his pocket watch, then put his hand through the window and honked the horn again.

"Is that really my grandfather?" Elliot whispered.

"Yes, indeed," said Mrs. Gibson. "And it seems he's a man who doesn't like to be kept waiting."

There was no time for breakfast. Elliot picked up Apollo and ran out to meet the stranger on the street. The man was standing with his back turned, impatiently tapping his fingers on the car roof. Elliot walked over and stood behind him for a few moments. The man did not seem to notice his presence.

"Err…Hello, sir. I'm Elliot Bade."

"Ah, finally!" The man turned around and studied Elliot with a pair of piercing blue eyes.

Elliot was immediately struck by how familiar the man's features were. Just like my mom's! he thought, as he gingerly took another step towards his grandfather.

"Tell me, how long does it take for a young lad like you to get out of bed and dress?" grumbled the man, then grabbed Elliot's hand and squeezed it between his bony fingers. Elliot guessed it was his grandfather's version of a handshake.

"Get in!" the man said abruptly and opened the car door.

Elliot hesitated. "We are going to the hospital, right?"

The man stopped and stared at the boy. "They didn't tell you, did they? Your mother is not doing too well. She's in an isolated ward where no visitors are allowed. There's no point of going to the hospital. We're going straight to my house, and you'll be staying with me until she gets better. Come now, we're late."

Elliot did not move. He felt a lump in his throat. "I have to stop at my house and pick up a few things… my books, toys…"

"Elliot, there's nothing left of your house. It burned down to the ground. Besides, you won't need books and toys where we're going. There are far more interesting things to keep you busy. Now, do get in."

Elliot climbed onto the front seat.

"Oh, by the way," the man said, motioning towards Apollo, "do you really need to bring that cat with you?"

"What do you mean? She's all I've got… no one else."

The old man just nodded and started the engine. Suddenly, Elliot heard a low growl behind him. The head of a massive dog loomed over the front seat.

Terrified, he tightened his grip around Apollo. The poor cat shuddered and let out a wailing meow. She tensed, ready to bolt.

"Down boy!" his grandfather said, and the dog immediately retreated. "That's Rupert. He doesn't like company," he added with a shrug and a wry smile.

Elliot glanced nervously over his shoulder. The dog was lying on the back seat. His lips were curled up, his fangs bared and dripping drool.

What a welcome! Elliot thought. He turned back to his grandfather. "I…I don't even know your name," he stammered. "Shall I call you granddad or…"

"Everybody calls me the Colonel. That'll do for now," the man said dryly as they pulled away from the curb.

· ◑ ·

The journey took forever. The Colonel did not say much. Most of the time he just stared ahead, occasionally muttering something to his dog. Elliot was in no mood to talk either. He was too busy feeling sorry for himself.

The farther they drove, the fewer cars they saw. Eventually, the road became a single country lane. It soon began to snake up a mountain, taking them higher and higher. The sky grew dark and the air cold.

Finally, they turned onto a graveled driveway and pulled up in front of what Elliot assumed was the Colonel's house. It stood there big and lonely, with nothing around it but pine trees. Elliot's heart sank even further.

They all got out of the car, and the Colonel led Elliot inside and up a creaky staircase to the attic. "This will be your bedroom," he said. "You can rest a little. I'll meet you downstairs for dinner in an hour. Try not to be late." He turned to leave, but stopped short of the door. They could hear Rupert prowling outside the closed door, his nails clicking on the wood floor.

The Colonel glanced back at Elliot. "Keep an eye on your cat. It's for her own safety." And with those words, he was gone.

Elliot put Apollo on the floor, and she immediately crept under the bed. He sat down, buried his head in his hands, and began to cry. It's all my fault, he thought.

If only he hadn't snuck out the night of the fire. If only he had stayed home. Instead, he had packed a bag with his telescope and a map of the constellations. He'd headed for the hills above their house to star gaze, perhaps pick out a new constellation, and check out the phase of the Moon. He knew his mother did not approve of his love of astronomy.

"Elliot, I wish you'd stop messing around with that telescope of yours. Spend more time with your friends. Be a normal kid!" she had said.

That was impossible to imagine. How could he be "normal" when he simply did not fit in? He was not one of those popular kids at school. Besides, what was wrong with his hobby? Why wouldn't she even come out and look at the Moon with him?

Every time he had asked her to, she had glanced the other way and fallen silent. "I just don't want to lose someone else to something that's two-hun-dred-and-fifty-thousand miles away," she had blurted out only a few nights ago, pointing at the pale crescent framed in their kitchen window. He still didn't understand what she had been talking about, but he wished he had listened to her anyway. He would have been at home with her when the fire had start-ed. He could have helped her get out of the house safely.

Elliot wiped away his tears with the back of his hand and looked at his watch. More than an hour had gone by. He washed his face and dragged himself downstairs to the dining room.

The Colonel was already there, seated at one end of a very long table. He pointed to the opposite end where Elliot's dinner was waiting, then continued eating. Elliot sat down and poked at his food. He wasn't hungry. Finally, the Colonel put his knife and fork down and stared at Elliot.

"Look, Elliot, I know you don't want to be here right now. I am not too comfortable about this situation myself. But we have to make it work somehow, the two of us."

"How come I never even knew I had a grandfather?" Elliot suddenly blurted out. "Why didn't someone tell me?"

The Colonel looked away and coughed nervously. "Your mother and I... we... let's just say... we haven't spoken in years. You'll have to ask her." He pushed his chair back, stood up, and walked over to Elliot. "Now, that you know you have a grandfather, allow the old man to introduce himself properly," he said and patted Elliot on the back. "Why don't we do that in my study?" he added. "Follow me."

Elliot nodded and managed a weak smile.

• ☽ •

The Colonel led the boy out of the dining room and through a long, dark corridor to his study. He produced a key from his pocket and unlocked the door. They entered a dimly lit room. Elliot froze. He was mesmerized by the rows upon rows of thick leather-bound books lining the walls. Maps of planets and star constellations hung above the fireplace. Elliot saw shelves laden with fantastic tools and instruments, and his heart skipped a beat. He recognized some of them: telescopes, armillary globes, compasses, sextants. And then, in the darkest corner of the study, he noticed a tall glass cabinet. Inside was something quite remarkable. Elliot could not believe his eyes. It was a spacesuit!

"In case you're wondering," the old man said, "that spacesuit's mine."

Elliot was speechless. "You were an astronaut?" he finally exclaimed. The Colonel nodded. Now Elliot wanted to ask his grandfather a million questions and hear all his stories.

The Colonel led Elliot to a large mahogany desk and motioned for him to sit down. Elliot held his breath as he waited for his grandfather to speak.

"First, I was a fighter pilot," the old man began, pointing to an old black and white photograph. "Then I was a geologist. And finally, a job came along where I could both fly the skies and explore what was under my feet." He walked to a nearby cabinet and slowly unlocked it. He took out a small glass box and carefully placed it before Elliot.

"This," he began, "is an ancient Moon Rock. All Moon Rocks are extremely valuable, but this one is even more so. It's four-and-a-half-billion years old. As old as Earth…some say the Moon and the Earth were once one…until a meteor blasted them apart."

Spellbound, Elliot stared at the rock. Its mineral crystals caught the light and twinkled like little stars. He was looking at a real piece of the Moon! His fingers began to twitch. It was almost as if the rock had some invisible power. Like a magnet, it drew Elliot's hand towards it.

Moon Globe

"Can I hold it?"

The Colonel quickly put the rock back in the box, closed the lid, and put the box back in the cabinet. "No, Elliot. It's too valuable. A few of the ones we brought back have already mysteriously disappeared. It's not a toy."

The Colonel had barely finished speaking when the telephone rang. "Don't touch anything!" he said as he left the study.

Elliot looked at the cabinet where the Moon Rock was and felt his heart skip another beat. His grandfather had left the key in the lock! The temptation was so great that he didn't hesitate for long. He quickly opened the cabinet, grabbed the box, and took out the rock. It was heavier than he had imagined. The sound of the Colonel's footsteps just outside the door made him jump. Elliot quickly slipped the rock into his pocket and returned the empty box to the cabinet.

"The hospital called," the Colonel said, entering the room. "Your mother's condition is still very serious."

"Is she going to...?" Elliot began, but could not bring himself to say the terrible word that he'd been thinking of since the night of the fire.

"Only the future will tell," replied his grandfather with a solemn face. Elliot was not sure, but for a second he thought the Colonel's voice sounded a little softer. "Come on, young man, it's been a long day. Time for both of us to get some rest."

Caught up in thoughts about his mother, Elliot forgot about the rock in his pocket and went up to bed.

• ◯ •

At some point in the middle of the night, Elliot awoke to a strange crackling noise above his head. He saw tiny lightning rods dancing all over the room, and before he could blink, four sword-carrying warriors appeared before him. Clad in ancient armor, faces hidden behind gas masks, they stood motionless around his bed. The raspy sound of their labored breathing filled the room. One of them removed a small, silver ball from under his breastplate and tossed it in the air. Instead of falling to the ground, the shiny object hovered above their heads. The sphere became transparent, and a green flame

16

flickered to life and then became an unwavering emerald beam. It scanned the room slowly until it came to rest on the frightened boy.

Suddenly, a rush of icy cold wind swept down from the ceiling. With a thunderous crash, more heavily armed men appeared. Brandishing their weapons, they immediately fell upon the warriors around Elliot's bed. He watched in terror as a fierce battle broke out between the two groups right there, in the middle of his room!

"Wake up!" he cried. He rubbed his eyes. But the men were still there! The sound of metal crashing on metal was deafening. Someone grabbed him and lifted him up with great force. Before he knew it, Elliot felt like he was being sucked into a giant wind tunnel. He spun faster and faster until everything became a blur. Then, as quickly as it had begun, all was quiet. He was lying in bed, as if nothing had happened.

Exhausted from fear, he quickly drifted back to sleep.

· ☽ ·

When Elliot opened his eyes, the room was still very dark, except for a streak of pale blue light coming from the window. But something was not quite right. The window! It was much bigger than it had been. There was no glass or window frame, and heavy velvet drapes hung on either side. He strained his eyes in the darkness. The walls looked different, too. The wallpaper was gone. No wood floor either. Just slabs of granite.

He was lying in a huge four-poster bed with intricate designs carved all over its wooden frame.

Is that a canopy over my bed? I must be still dreaming, he thought, yet he felt strangely awake. He sat up and swung his feet around until they touched the cold floor. Something rolled off his lap and fell to the floor with a loud thud. He reached down and picked it up. The Moon Rock!

Cautiously, Elliot stood up, walked over to the big window, and peered outside. Instead of the silhouettes of trees he had seen the night before, outside lay a city. A city like no other he had ever seen.

Coursing through it was a misty, meandering river. The sky was still very dark, but he could see the outlines of large stone buildings, topped with

turrets and towers that disappeared into thick fog. A maze of cobbled streets glistened in the feeble light of the street lanterns. But there was not a single soul around. Nothing stirred. The eerie silence made him shiver.

Then he heard a sound.

At first it was very faint, but it grew increasingly louder and closer. The sound reminded Elliot of a foghorn. Suddenly, the beam of a bright search light pierced the fog and bounced off the walls of the buildings. Out of the fog, like a giant lopsided blimp, emerged an enormous whale. Elliot gasped in disbelief. The creature slowly glided through the air with a gondola attached to its underbelly. As it passed, Elliot noticed it had a number stenciled on its massive side. The whale crossed the space above the river and vanished into the fog on the other side. The foghorn sound gradually faded away. Elliot stood and waited, hoping for the bizarre airship to reappear. A hush fell over the city again.

What next? Elliot wondered. And, almost as if his thoughts had been read, he heard the unmistakable sound of footsteps. Someone was quickly approaching the bedroom, or bedchamber, or wherever he was. Elliot looked around for a place to hide. He jumped behind the curtain and held his breath. The footsteps grew louder. Then came a thump, followed by a piercing squeal of an animal in pain.

A horrible, raspy voice hissed, "You clumsy fool! Watch where you step or be trampled like the bug that you are!" The voice dropped to a whisper, and Elliot could not make out what it was saying.

With the flick of a switch, a light came on.

"Where is the boy?" asked the same raspy voice. "He must be here somewhere. Go forth! Fetch!"

Elliot carefully peered from behind the curtain. Something lunged at him. Inches from his face, hovering in mid air, was the ugliest, scariest creature imaginable. It looked like a lizard with rough, scaly skin, but it had crablike legs. It flailed about, scratching at the curtain. Its gaping mouth, full of long, sharp teeth, opened and closed in a terrible bone-crunching frenzy. The beast had a collar around its neck with a leash attached to it. Elliot stood there, frozen with fear, unable to move or make a sound. Suddenly, an invisible hand yanked hard on the leash. The creature choked and fell on the floor, gasping for breath.

"Pray come forward, dear boy," said the hoarse voice, now full of assurance. "Fear us not. You are amongst friends."

Elliot did not move. "Look, I know this is a dream," he replied. "But I don't think I like it anymore. Can it stop, please? Can I wake up and go? I've got to return the Moon Rock, before the Colonel..."

The curtain was pulled back, exposing Elliot fully. Before him stood a scrawny man dressed in red velvety breeches and top. The man's ashy face was covered with hundreds of wrinkles, and he was wearing a big, white wig. His little yellow eyes sparkled with amusement as he stared at Elliot. Slowly, his lips stretched into a broad smile.

"I assure you, a dream this is not, dear Elliot," he said. He casually glanced at the boy's hand, and his smile became even broader.

"As for your rock, fret not your precious head! Of course, your grand-papa shall have it back. All in due course. But firstly, pray allow me to welcome you to our city. You, my boy, are the most important of guests."

Elliot looked down at the creature still sputtering on the floor and then back to the old man. He shook his head. "No, this is definitely a dream!"

"Alas, you are mistaken," the man chuckled. "But if you prefer it that way, a dream it shall be. Now, pray permit me to introduce myself. I go by the name of Magnus DuBereux and bear the title of the Librarian of Time. As such, I govern this city. But enough said, for we must make haste. Pray be dressed and prepare to meet my Chancellors. Vergil!"

The Librarian unleashed the creature, snapped his fingers, and the nasty creature obediently scurried away into the darkest corner of the chamber. It returned, carrying what appeared to be a folded piece of clothing in its mouth, and sat like a dog in front of the boy. "Kindly proceed," said the Librarian, and noticing Elliot's hesitation, added, "Do not be alarmed. The little savage is under my control. Upon my word, he shall not harm you."

Elliot cautiously took the clothing from the beast's mouth and unfolded it. It was a silk-hooded robe. He put it over his pajamas and slipped on the leather sandals the creature pushed towards his feet. Surprisingly, everything fit.

"I must say, you look just right for our place now. Most definitely you appear as one of us, dear Elliot," said the Librarian approvingly.

"But, how... how do you know my name?"

"Ah, you'll be surprised how much I know about you. Much more than your name." He clapped his hands. The creature hopped into his arms and began to purr like a cat. The Librarian turned and walked away, petting and nuzzling the monster lovingly.

Elliot followed the pair out of the chamber and into a dimly lit corridor that led them to a spiral staircase. They started to climb. Elliot was amazed at how quickly the Librarian moved. The old man bounded up the steps with such ease that Elliot had trouble keeping up. Finally, they reached a landing, walked down another lengthy corridor, and entered a large hall.

Ornate tapestries hung from the walls, a thick maroon carpet covered the floor, and dazzling chandeliers spun in circles above their heads. The Librarian led Elliot to a chair in front of a long polished wood table. Behind it stood three nervous-looking figures. It was only after the old man had taken his seat that the Chancellors sat down.

"Elliot Bade," DuBereux said, breaking the solemn silence, "it is an honor to welcome you to Great Nidor! Few have ventured to the South Pole and fewer still to this ancient city of ours."

"Is Great Nidor in Antarctica?" Elliot's eyes grew wide. The Chancellors politely stifled their laughter while DuBereux shook his head.

"I speak of a different South Pole, much colder and more desolate than yours," the old man said, as he opened a large book lying on the table in front of him. Carefully, he dipped a quill pen into a tiny pot of green ink. "I shall now officially enter your name into the visitor's ledger!"

"Am I your sole visitor?" Elliot asked as he stared at the book's blank page.

DuBereux nodded and grinned sheepishly. "Admittedly, we stand submerged in eternal twilight, well-concealed from prying eyes."

"What do you mean?"

"Great Nidor lies in the valley of Kyth, and, I hasten to add, it is a valley of unique position. Kyth is to be found at the bottom of the deepest crater that has deigned to pockmark our barren world. The crater's depth is of astounding measure. But there is more." The Librarian paused and twirled the quill between his fingers. "You see, dear child, above our city is an icy dome, and the crater's walls are sheets of frozen water! The Sun's hot rays can never reach us, nor melt the ice deposits on the Other Side."

"Excuse me, but what is this 'Other Side?'" Elliot asked.

The Chancellors raised their eyebrows.

"Why, dear child, it is the side you cannot see!" Magnus DuBereux's eyes twinkled with delight. "Often you have looked up to the sky at our pale face seeing a mere half of what there is," he intoned and waited for the boy to guess the rest of his riddle.

Elliot stood with furrowed brow, searching for the answer. Suddenly he gasped. "The Other Side... you mean the Far Side! The Far Side of the Moon?"

"Clever boy!"

"I'm on the Moon! But... how... how's this possible?"

"How?!? The rock my dear boy, the rock! The Moon Rock made it all possible. And allow me to tell you that, had we not acted fast enough, this rock would not have stayed in your possession for very long."

Elliot stared at the rock in his hand in disbelief. "But, it's just...a rock!"

"That rock, dear child, holds the key to our future," said the Librarian. "It may not look like anything special, but I assure you, it has cost many souls their lives. It would have also cost you yours, had we not the good fortune to intervene. And intervene we did. Pray remember what befell you in your bedchamber."

Elliot shuddered. How could he ever forget!

"My men fought bravely to prevent your most certain death. We plucked you and the rock from the clutches of pure evil. We saved you, and with that, our Future!"

The Librarian leaned back in his chair and proudly glanced at the Chancellors. They all nodded their heads and gave him a loud round of applause. He beamed and looked back at Elliot.

"Now, let me introduce you to those who help me govern this city and its subjects." The Librarian rose up and waved the quill in the air. "To my right here is Chancellor Cadogan," he began, pointing to an extremely fat man, whose little eyes kept darting up and down, left to right. "He ensures that our transport —our traffic on the ground and in the sky— runs properly. All praise to him, for we have not had a Whale strike for a good, long while." He waited for his Chancellors to finish clapping their hands

before continuing. "And to my left is Chancellor Morana, in charge of security matters." DuBereux turned to a painfully thin woman who was dressed in shiny black leather. She sat upright, expressionless. Her icy stare bore into Elliot, and he instinctively lowered his gaze.

"Needless to say, we have our enemies," the Librarian continued. "Bandits who like to call themselves Defiers who persistently try to undermine my authority by wreaking havoc on our great city. The lies they spread have poisoned many minds and ruined good and honest lives. Chancellor Morana's efforts to clean the streets of those wicked dissemblers have been extremely successful! The good lady has forced most of them to go underground... where, of course, she continues to hunt them. My latest intelligence reports assure me that very few are left." The Librarian looked extremely pleased as those at the table showed their appreciation with more applause. Walking slowly behind the table, the Librarian appeared to grow taller. "And next to her is Refuggio, the Chancellor of Gravitation. As you probably know, my little friend, gravity here allows objects to move about... to levitate. We, of course, do not like to encourage free levitation because it can easily cause chaos and disorder. Chancellor Refuggio makes sure levitation is controlled, most properly monitored, and that our subjects follow the rules of the land."

Elliot looked at the tiny, bespectacled man with spiky hair who was grinning at him.

"But I don't understand," Elliot said. "How can you control gravity?"

Refuggio's face became serious. He nervously glanced at the Librarian, who gave him a nod.

"Take a look at your wrist," said Chancellor Refuggio in a high-pitched voice. Elliot pulled up his sleeve and found a metal bracelet covered in strange-looking dials locked around his wrist. Somehow he had failed to notice it before.

"Everyone here in Great Nidor has to wear one of these," the Chancellor continued, lifting his hand to show his own bracelet. "Through these devices we can control gravity. We can increase it, decrease it, or completely stop it at will. We can do that by..." He stopped mid-sentence.

Magnus DuBereux had placed his hand on the Chancellor's shoulder. He playfully tickled the Chancellor's stubby nose with the quill. "Of course, we do not allow the regular citizens the ability to adjust their bracelets themselves. That would be far too dangerous. Only a few trusted ones can be given that privilege." Elliot suddenly remembered how easily the old Librarian had climbed the stairs, two steps at a time. He had decreased the force of gravity, the boy thought, studying his own bracelet. The dials on his were moving very slowly.

"Well, time is precious. We should not waste any more of it," the Librarian said. All the Chancellors stood up.

"Sir," Elliot said, trying to carefully choose his words. "I'm honored to be your guest, but…but I really need to get back now. It's not just the rock. You see, my mother…"

"Ah, yes, your poor mother." DuBereux's voice was suddenly full of concern. "She is in hospital, is she not? So devastatingly sad! Naturally, you want to be with her, the good son that you are. And what, pray, do you think you can do for her?" The old man's face was right in front of Elliot's now. "You may go if you so wish. But perhaps you shall change your mind if I were to tell you," the Librarian had lowered his voice to a whisper, "that by staying here in Great Nidor, you shall have a much greater chance of helping your beloved mother."

"How?" Elliot could feel his heart racing. "I'll do anything, anything!"

"Are you staying?"

"Yes!"

"Clever boy. Now, pray, come along." DuBereux smiled. He put his arm around the boy's shoulder and directed him out of the hall. Vergil and all the Chancellors trailed behind them. They climbed more stairs and stepped out onto a roof-top terrace.

It took a few moments for Elliot's eyes to adjust to the sudden brightness that greeted them. Before them, suspended in mid air, was the most amazing airship he had ever seen.

It was shaped like an egg and plated in gold. Thick chains anchored it to the terrace's floor and golden cables extended from its roof. He looked up to see where they went, and he could only gasp at what he saw next. The cables were attached to the underbelly of a whale! Just like the one he had seen earlier! The massive creature above their heads swayed gently, bobbing up and down.

"Behold my modest vessel," the Librarian said.

He escorted Elliot down a red carpet that stretched to a gilded staircase and on up to the airship's bejeweled door. The Chancellors and Vergil scurried after them.

The inside of the craft was even more impressive than the outside. The walls were made of dark wood and covered with exquisite ornaments. A fireplace blazed at the far end of the cabin. In the middle there was a big table laden with gold dishes filled with exotic food. The sight of the feast made Elliot's mouth water.

"Do help yourself to some refreshments whilst we prepare for take off," said the Librarian, gesturing towards the table.

Chancellor Cadogan was the first to reach for the food. Elliot watched in astonishment as Cadogan quickly demolished entire plates of it. Elliot grabbed a few pastries and rushed to a nearby window, eager to watch the take off. Once the door was closed and the chains unhooked, the airship slowly began to climb.

He was scared but excited at the same time. It seemed strangly quiet and calm with no sound of engines and no turbulence.

They glided silently, very low, just above the roofs of the buildings. It was still fairly dark and somewhat foggy outside, but it was clear enough for Elliot to admire the amazing spread of the city below, with all its watchtowers, buttress walls, battlements, and courtyards.

A myriad of canals flowed into a big winding river. Bridges spanned the waterways. Gigantic water wheels slowly churned away along the river's wide banks.

"They provide our city with power," explained the Librarian. "All that water is from the ice deposits above."

"I'd love to take a walk down there," whispered Elliot. "Can I?"

He turned to DuBereux.

"Why, of course, my dear boy," the Librarian replied and patted him on the back. "But we have important work to do first."

The craft started to descend towards a hill in the heart of the city. Three adjoining structures towered on top of the hill. The craft gently touched down next to a paved stairway that led to the entrance of the first structure.

Two menacing-looking creatures holding spears stood motionlessly on either side of the steps. Their scaly skin glistened despite the meager light.

"The Library's Sentries," said DuBereux, leading the boy out of the craft and towards the terrifying guards. "They are fierce and strong, but exceptionally loyal and completely under my control."

Elliot cautiously walked between the guards and followed Magnus DuBereux's effortless climb up the paved stairway. Elliot was certain the Librarian was using his gravity bracelet again. Then he noticed the statue. It stood on a large stone pedestal in front of the building. One arm was lifted, pointing forward. As they approached it, Elliot realized the monument's features resembled those of the Librarian himself. The old man followed Elliot's gaze and smiled bashfully.

"Ah, the grateful citizens of Nidor decided to show their respect by erecting a likeness of me, leading them towards a bright Future. And this, Elliot," he said, turning and gesturing to the building ahead, "is the Library of Time. The most important library in existence. It has three wings: the Wing of the Past, of the Present, and of the Future. I suggest we start with the first one. "

He led Elliot through the main entrance to a massive wooden door, which he unlocked and pushed open with his foot. The door's rusty hinges creaked loudly, and the smell of mold and rot wafted into their faces. The Wing of the Past lay before them, silent and dark. The only source of light was the one now coming through the open doorway. It revealed row after row of shelves reaching from floor to ceiling, stacked with books. Elliot had never seen so many books before! Cautiously, he stepped over the threshold. Giant cobwebs and thick layers of dust covered everything. Ancient tomes lay open and abandoned, their pages torn and decayed. It looked like the place had been deserted in a great hurry.

"What's in all these books?" asked Elliot.

"Lies and misinformation," replied the Librarian. "History books full of inaccurate accounts of bygone days. Boring nonsense, for which I have no patience."

"What kind of nonsense?" asked Elliot, puzzled by the Librarian's words.

"The kind that accounts for all people's pasts." The Librarian scowled and pointed at the towering shelves. "Every single life story imaginable can

be found here. Histories of individuals from across the Universe told and retold, until no one can be certain of what is true."

"And no one reads them anymore?"

"We do not encourage visits to this wing. These dusty archives contain so little truth that they can only give our citizens wrong ideas and confuse their minds. One has no need to look back at the past!"

"But how can people live without books? Without... knowledge?" Elliot asked.

"Ah, there are far better and more interesting ways to gain knowledge, believe me, my little friend!" exclaimed the old man. "Pray, allow me to show you our next wing, and you shall see for yourself."

Elliot watched the Librarian lock the door and thought, What if one of the books in there contains my own family's story and secrets?

He might be able to find out what happened between his mother and the Colonel and learn the reason for their silence.

As if the Librarian had read Elliot's thoughts, he said, "Regrettably, there is so much sadness and bitterness in one's past. Often it is best to forget. Let bygones be bygones, Elliot. I believe where you come from they have a curious expression. Something about spilt water, or was it wine...?"

"Milk," replied Elliot. Oddly, his mother had uttered this saying many times over the years. "The saying is 'No point crying over spilt milk.'"

"Precisely so!" The Librarian laughed and quickly led Elliot to the adjoining building.

· ◑ ·

Unlike the Wing of the Past, the door to the Present was unlocked. Together they walked into a great hall that was brightly lit and buzzing with activity. The whole place resembled a giant control room. Rows of shiny metal cabinets filled the large space, and strange instruments were mounted on top of the cabinets. There were dials, gauges, and levers of different shapes and sizes. Large tubular screens hung from the ceiling with images flickering on them. Silver uniformed operators sat in tall swivel chairs fixed to gliding floor rails. They quickly moved from one monitor to the next. The Librarian motioned to one of them to step down and invited Elliot to take the operator's seat. Then he hopped on the little platform by Elliot's side. They slid along the rails, past the cabinets, and stopped in front of one of the monitors.

The Librarian punched a few keys, and a familiar image appeared. Elliot saw himself lying on the bed in the chamber. He watched himself get up, walk over to the window, and jump behind the curtain. He watched DuBereux and Vergil appear on the screen. Just as Vergil lunged at the curtain where Elliot stood hiding, the film froze.

As Elliot stared at his own terrified and contorted face on the screen, he heard a strange snickering sound. He turned and saw that Vergil had joined them. He felt a surge of hatred for the creature.

"Ah, the beauty of modern technology," murmured the Librarian in a dreamy voice, as he nuzzled his monstrous pet. "That was you, not too long ago, my boy. Bear witness that there is no hiding in my city. We have monitoring devices everywhere, every place imaginable. Marvelous, is it not?"

Elliot was not convinced. He remembered his mother once scolding him for having trained his telescope on a neighbor's window.

"But… that's spying, sir," he whispered, unable to take his eyes off the screen.

"Oh, I would not call it spying. I call it gathering of information," the old man replied. "Pray, tell me, how can I govern this city without knowing what occurs at any given moment? We live in dangerous times, dear boy. We have enemies, as I told you earlier, who hide amongst us, spread their lies, and try to harm the good citizens of Great Nidor. They call themselves Defiers, but personally, I would much rather call them Deceivers, for they are masters of deception. These shameless liars would say and do anything to try and win my people over. Thus, we need to watch over everyone. Most people understand it is for their own safety and do not complain about it. We offer great rewards to those who willingly come forward with information about the Defiers. We encourage them to observe one another and be vigilant. Why, it is in their best interest!"

"They must visit this wing more often, then," Elliot said. "The good citizens, I mean."

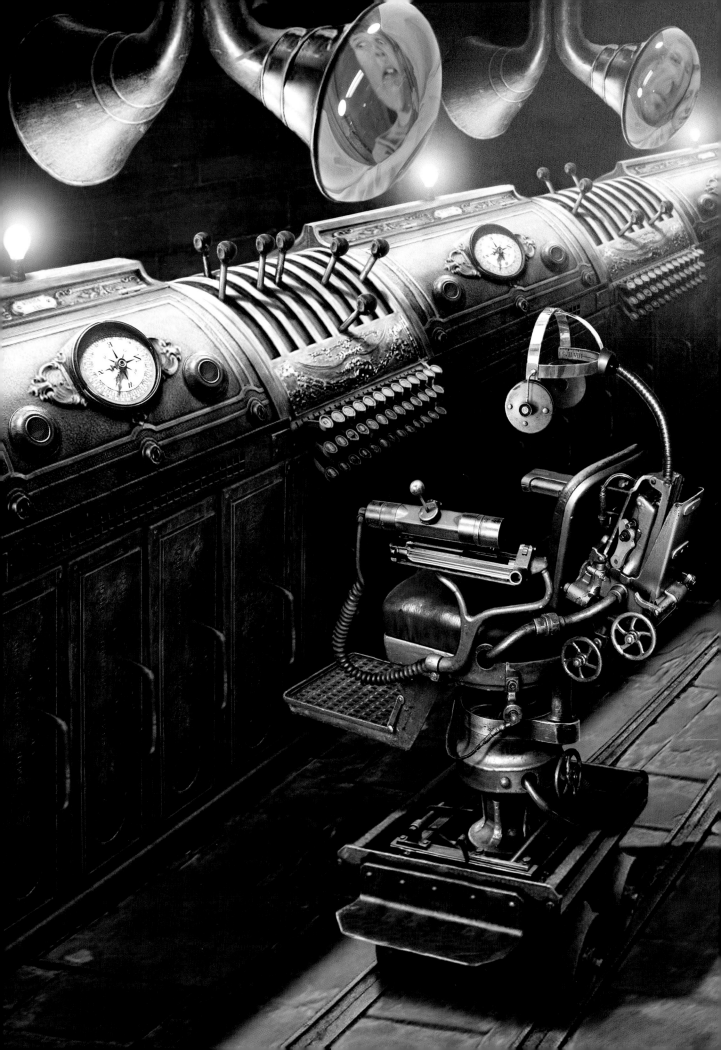

"Indeed, they most certainly do. But, alas, not as many as I would desire. Some still feel uncomfortable looking at themselves this way. Give them time, I say. They shall learn and grow accustomed to it. Now, pray, let us proceed. The most important wing awaits our company."

As they were leaving, Elliot caught a glimpse of a girl's face on the last monitor. A pair of haunting blue eyes stared straight at the camera, and an icy shiver ran down Elliot's spine. Before he could look again, DuBereux flicked a switch, and the screen went black.

"Who was that?" asked Elliot.

"No one of importance," the Librarian hastily replied as he quickly ushered Elliot out of the brightness of the Present and back into the dusky light outside. There, he let Vergil go, and to Elliot's great relief, the creature quickly slunk into the shadows and was gone.

· ● ·

The Librarian and Elliot made their way to a building surrounded by a dried-up moat. Elliot saw the raised drawbridge and the ominous spikes along the walls of the Wing of the Future. Two Sentries quickly lowered the bridge so they could walk across to the inner courtyard on the other side. A jewel-encrusted door towered in front of them. The lock was an intricate mechanism with an indentation of a hand in the middle of it.

"Well," said the Librarian, "there it is, Elliot. The very reason you are here today. Only you and you alone can open that door."

"Me?" Elliot took a step back.

"Yes, you, dear child! And the rock that you carry. I told you it holds the key to the Future. I spoke not in jest."

Suddenly, the hand imprint on the lock began to throb, emitting a low pulsating sound.

"See that! The door has sensed your heartbeat! It heralds your presence, for the rock has truly chosen you as its key bearer." DuBereux cupped Elliot's chin and looked into his eyes.

Elliot took the rock out of his pocket, hesitated for a moment, and then offered it to DuBereux. "Here. Take it."

The Librarian shook his head. "If only it were so simple. A spell was cast, a touch of magic if you like, on that rock. Only an innocent, a child, can make the key inside work again."

Elliot looked at the rock and was suddenly terribly frightened. The lock mechanism groaned, sputtered, and fell silent. The Librarian glanced at the door and frowned. "I wish this door had been opened sooner," he said, his voice now full of bitterness. "My son would be alive today if it had," he whispered, choking back his tears. "I would have seen what cruel fate awaited him ahead of time. I could have saved his life!" The Librarian was now openly sobbing. Elliot felt a lump rise in his throat, too. He reached out and squeezed the Librarian's hand.

"I would hate to see you lose the only person you so dearly love," added the Librarian.

Elliot's heart skipped a beat. "You mean my mom?"

The Librarian nodded. "Indeed, my boy. Your mother shall be well once more. Her sadness and suffering mended. Open the Future and think of all the good we can do. Bad things will never have to happen, for we shall know how to prevent them. Our enemies shall be defeated. All our dreams will come true. Wouldn't you like to journey into the Future, see what it holds for you, and change it as you please?"

"You can change my Future?"

"Oh, I most certainly can, my dear little friend. It is so simple. Once inside, you shall see everything that awaits you. Anything that is not to your liking, I shall correct. Anything your heart desires, I shall make yours. Your wishes shall be my most imperative of commands."

Elliot's head was beginning to spin. I'll be with Mom again! he thought excitedly. We'll have tons of money, live anywhere we choose, do whatever we want… I'll be the most popular boy at school, have all the coolest gadgets and toys, the best telescopes, even an observatory of my own… I'll be an astronaut one day, just like the Colonel!

"Okay, let's open it. Show me what to do!" he cried eagerly. The lock was once again pulsating with great intensity.

"Not so fast," said DuBereux with a smile. "First, we need to extract the key hidden in the rock. It is a very complicated procedure. Pray, follow me." He led Elliot back over the drawbridge. They had only taken a few steps when the old man bent down and picked up what looked like long leather straps lying on the stone floor.

"Steady now!" he cried.

Suddenly, the ground beneath Elliot's feet moved, and they were lifted up into the air.

"Are we levitating?" he asked excitedly. Was this zero gravity?

"No, we are not. But he is," said the Librarian, pointing down.

Elliot looked at his feet.

They were standing on the back of a giant winged creature that had been so well-camouflaged that he had failed to notice it. A flying stingray! DuBereux pulled on the reins, and they took off very quickly. The stingray flew much faster than the whale. At first, Elliot was a little frightened since he had nothing to hold onto, but the stingray's flight was so smooth, he started to enjoy the ride. Once again they flew very low, above the deserted streets, weaving under and over the arches of countless bridges, skimming the water, and cutting through the mist. It felt like they were on a giant surfboard, riding on vapors and gusts of wind. The Librarian seemed to be in full control of the creature, navigating it with ease between the buildings. After a particularly tricky turn, the man tightened the reins, and the stingray glided to a halt, gently touching down on a narrow cobbled street. The creature immediately disguised itself to match the surface and became invisible.

They stood alone in the cold light of the street lanterns, in front of what looked like a very tall clock tower. It was shrouded in fog. Their steps echoed as they walked over to the tower's entrance. DuBereux knocked on the heavy door and waited. With a soft click it swung open, but there was no one to greet them on the other side. Once across the threshold, a tiny cubicle of an elevator whisked them up. Its cage doors opened to reveal a dimly lit room with a giant clock mechanism in the middle of it. Elliot looked around in amazement. Weights on pulleys were moving up and down, big brass pendulums were swinging right to left, and huge cogwheels were turning slowly with hollow ticking sounds.

"So, this is the boy!" came a high-pitched voice from behind the clock's face.

With a rattling of chains, a metal swing-basket appeared out of the darkness. It slid noisily towards Elliot. In it sat an old man so small, he was almost the size of a baby. On top of his head, like a crown, he wore a sinister metal contraption made of clocks, dials, and magnifying glasses. Elliot stepped back and bumped into DuBereux.

"Meet Boniface, the Clocksmyth of Nidor," said the Librarian. "Pray, follow his instructions."

The little man motioned Elliot towards a battered reclining seat covered with cranks and dials. It reminded Elliot of a dentist's chair, and he gave an involuntary shudder.

"Will this hurt?" he asked, suddenly frightened.

"Come, come, now! A coward you are not!" DuBereux scoffed. "Pray, sit yourself down, child!"

Reluctantly, Elliot did as he was told.

"Hold the rock in your right hand and lift it up," the Clocksmyth said in a hushed voice.

A rusty metal claw extended from a mechanism on the side of the chair and locked with a snap around the boy's wrist, immobilizing his hand.

"Now, open your hand," ordered the Clocksmyth and started to position his magnifying glasses around the rock. He grunted and shifted in his rusty cradle, until finally he was satisfied with his adjustments. "Close your eyes, and hold your breath. Don't move a muscle, or you'll lose your hand!"

Eyes closed tight, Elliot could hear the little man muttering something under his breath. He felt the rock move in his hand and heard a hissing sound like that of water sizzling on a hot surface. Steam rose up his nose and washed over his face, but he held his breath. Then he felt a sharp jab, and his palm began to throb. It quickly grew very warm and sticky. With a loud clunk, the manacle unlocked and freed his wrist.

"Good, we've got the key," Elliot heard the Clocksmyth say. "You can open your eyes now."

Elliot did. The room was swimming. He had to focus extremely hard in order to see his trembling hand. He gasped. The rock had vanished. In its place was a round, flat object in the middle of his palm. It resembled a clock, with moving needles for hands and strange signs for numbers. Carefully he

touched it, then rubbed it gingerly with his finger. Whatever it was, it was embedded into his skin! And yet he felt no pain or discomfort from it being there.

The Librarian stepped forward. "Bravo! Excellent work! You shall be well rewarded for your labor, Boniface."

Elliot jumped from the chair, fear in his eyes. "What's this thing in my hand? What happened to the rock?" he cried.

"Why, it is the key, my dear boy!" said DuBereux, unable to hide his excitement. "All that is needed now is for you to put your precious hand on the lock, and the Future will be ours! Ease your mind of all concern, for the key will disappear after that."

Elliot stared at this strangest of keys.

"What about the rock? How am I going to explain all this to my grandfather?"

"We shall worry about that later." The Librarian chuckled good-heartedly. "Plenty of Moon Rocks around here, dear boy! He shall never know the difference. Come, my dear child! We have cause for celebration." He grabbed Elliot's hand and rushed him to the elevator.

"Your Librarianship, don't forget about the extra precaution you requested," murmured the Clocksmyth after them. "Sir, it's there now and most dangerous!"

Elliot thought he saw anger in DuBereux's eyes as he glanced back, but the swing-basket had already disappeared into the darkness.

· ◐ ·

Down on the street, they were met by a group of armored guards. They reminded Elliot of the Library's Sentries, only these guards were of another, more frightful-looking breed. Very much like centaurs, they had the lower body of a four-legged beast and the torso of a broad-shouldered and extremely muscular ape-man. They stomped and pranced, while their tiny captain hovered in the air, mounted on the back of a manatee. Suddenly, something leapt into DuBereux's arms. With a start, Elliot realized it was none other than Vergil. The creature began to whisper urgently in his master's ear. Elliot heard the words "Defiers," "Leader," "Captured," but not much else.

"Why," DuBereux frowned, "is not Morana dealing with it?"

Vergil shook his head and whispered some more. The Librarian now looked annoyed.

"Upon my word," he said as he turned towards Elliot. "A very important matter needs my immediate attention. I shall have the great pleasure of adding someone very special to my collection of prisoners. What, with that and the key, it seems there shall be cause for a double celebration today! We must leave at once."

Vergil muttered something else under his breath. DuBereux stood there for a moment, then gravely nodded his head. "You are, indeed, right," he said. "It may not be a pretty sight for our honorable guest to witness. Alas, it is such unsavory business when a Defier finally surrenders." He paused and shuddered. "My dear boy, pray, forgive me. I am afraid you cannot come with me. Perchance you may like to take a brief walk through the city with Vergil and the guards? I believe that was something you wished to do."

Elliot nodded excitedly. "Yes, please!"

"Good," said DuBereux and before the boy knew what was happening, the Librarian had handed Vergil over to him. "We shall meet at the Library of Time, my friend," said DuBereux and snapped his fingers. The well-concealed stingray rose immediately from the pavement, and with the Librarian on its back, it swiftly disappeared down the dark alleyway.

"Ugh!" cried Elliot, immediately dropping the slimy crustacean to the ground. He would have preferred the Librarian as his guide through Great Nidor, not this horrid monster.

"Time's short! We must go, yes!" Vergil turned abruptly to the guards, giving his command in a deep and rather gruff voice. Elliot was so startled to hear the creature speak with such great a force that he stood frozen in his tracks.

"Move! 'Tis not safe to stand in one place for long, no," DuBereux's servant bellowed.

The guards formed a tight circle around Elliot and fell into a march. The noise of their stomping hooves reverberated off the surrounding buildings. The small but formidable convoy walked like this for a while, occasionally passing a lone figure in the otherwise deserted streets. Elliot could not help

Whale Dispatcher

but notice how the sight of his escorts made these citizens of Great Nidor lower their gaze and scurry away. He did not have time to think about this for long. Something else had caught his attention.

The convoy had led him into a vast, open market square where an enormous hangar-like structure reared up high into sky. It took Elliot a few moments to realize what purpose the building served. It was a Whale depot! The tails of a few whales were sticking out of the gigantic doorways. Moored to towering wooden scaffolds, the whales patiently waited, while handfuls of passengers embarked and disembarked from their gondolas. Heavy cargo crates were being loaded and unloaded by the minute. A sickly purplish light was breaking through the fog now, and it gave Elliot a better view of this surreal world. A strange figure slowly hobbled past them. It carried a bizarre-looking apparatus on its back, which made muffled horn-like sounds at regular intervals. Puzzled, Elliot stared at it.

" 'Tis a Whale Dispatcher, see," offered Vergil. "Talks to them whales, yes. Navigates 'em in and out. Makes sure them beasties don't make no noise, no."

"Noise?"

"Them whales like to sing, you see. Whale song's public nuisance, disturbs the peace and quiet of the citizens, yes, yes."

Elliot frowned as he stood and listened. Great Nidor was indeed a very silent place. Perhaps too quiet.

"Them whistling and howling helps our enemy, yes. Not too long ago, 'twas was their wicked way of sending coded messages, you see," Vergil added as he steered Elliot and the guards between rows of market stalls. The vendors stiffly bowed their heads and some even kneeled before the passing entourage. For the first time since he had arrived, Elliot was seeing real signs of life. But the overwhelming sadness of the city and its citizens was beginning to bother him. Everyone he walked past looked anxious and harried. Nobody was stopping to talk to anyone. A few gave him curious looks, and Elliot saw fear in their eyes.

"How come I don't see any kids here?" he suddenly asked Vergil.

"Children don't go out, no."

"Why?" asked Elliot.

" 'Tis too dangerous, you see."

Just then a carriage stopped a few feet from them, and two little heads peered through its heavily curtained window. Elliot saw the children's eyes fall on him, and he immediately recognized the look on their faces. It was one of longing. One of them rather timidly waved at him. But before Elliot could wave back, someone inside the carriage pulled the children away from the window, then snapped the curtains shut.

"They are afraid of the Defiers, aren't they?"

"Afraid, yes, yes. They kidnap 'em, you see. Never to be seen again, no."

Elliot shook his head. He felt sorry for everyone in Great Nidor, but most of all for the children. And, with a surge of anger, he knew who was to blame.

These poor people won't have to live in fear once DuBereux's captured the Defiers, thought Elliot, rubbing the palm of his hand. And that shouldn't take too long. The key to the Future will see to that!

"Let's go back to the Library of Time," said Elliot. "I think I've seen enough."

• ☽ •

They reached the harbor and quickly made their way up alongside the big river. Without warning, arrows began to fly through the air. Elliot heard Vergil shout "Ambush!" and, with their shields held high, the guards immediately formed a circle around him. Seconds later, he felt the ground shift. Elliot looked down. He was standing on a round manhole cover.

Then, in a flash, the cover was gone. Screaming at the top of his lungs, he dropped feet first into complete darkness, landing with a thump on a slippery stone slope. Quickly, his fall became a harrowing slide. He was now on a rollercoaster ride down a wet chute, the narrow walls rushing past him at breakneck speed.

Soon the chute spat him out. He landed with a splash in slimy, icy cold water that smelt of sewer. Luckily the water was only knee-deep. There was just enough light for Elliot to be able to make out, with strained eyes, his surroundings. Wet and shivering, he was standing completely alone in the middle of some sort of an underground canal. Now what? he thought. Where do I go? He hesitated for a minute. No point standing here, waiting to be rescued, he told himself, trying to remain as calm as possible. He slowly started wading through the foul-smelling water. It didn't matter which way he went. He didn't know the way out anyway. He walked for a while, until a noise made him stop. Voices! Elliot was almost certain that he could hear voices coming from somewhere in the tunnel behind him. He turned around and saw the light of torches rapidly approaching. The voices were louder now.

"I told you it was the wrong hole, Albin," one of the voices said. "You should've dropped him few streets back."

"Yeah, yeah! It's always my fault!" responded another voice.

"C'mon fellas, hurry up. He could freeze down here," a third voice joined in.

"There he is!" they shouted together.

Torch lights shone on Elliot. Half-blinded by the strong beams of light, he squinted and held his breath. Waist deep in the murky water stood three enormous rats, dressed in rubber suits with matching helmets and goggles on their heads.

"Hi there! How was the fall? Enjoyable?" asked one of the rats, extending his paw. "I'm Albin, and these two are the twins, Andoni and Arkadi."

"Am I being kidnapped?" Elliot took a step back, his heart pounding.

"Kidnapped?" Albin pulled his goggles up. "Rubbish! What makes you think that?"

"You fell down the wrong hole, that's all," said Andoni.

"Albin's fault!" added Arkadi.

"No worries, it's all taken care of!" said Albin. "You just need to pedal a little bit farther to get there."

"Get where?" Elliot's eyes shifted suspiciously from one rat to another. They seemed friendly enough, but he was not about to let his guard down.

"Where? Always ask the same question, don't they?" Albin muttered to the other rats, then turned back to Elliot. "Where you had to go to in the first place."

"A few holes back from here, that is," said Andoni.

"Hole number three-one-five to be precise," added Arkadi.

Albin, who was obviously in charge, turned to the twins. "Hurry up, they are waiting for him!"

"Who's waiting for me?" Elliot cried with growing frustration.

"Sorry, don't have time to chit-chat," Albin grumbled, and he went back to shouting instructions at the other two rats.

Andoni and Arkadi disappeared into the dark tunnel, then re-emerged, pulling on a heavy rope. Elliot followed it with his eyes and saw it was tied to something that resembled a bicycle. The contraption hung from a long monorail high above their heads. It had pedals, a single seat, and handle-bars with headlights on them.

"Let's get him up, boys," barked Albin, clapping his hands. The three rats quickly scrambled and formed a shaky ladder with their bodies. Albin was on top. "Come on boy, hop on!" he shouted.

Elliot did not move.

"Look, I don't know who you are, but I am an important guest of Magnus DuBereux. And I demand you take me back to him immediately!"

"Friends with DuBereux, are you?" Albin remarked.

"Yeah, we're friends. Take me back to him, and I'll make sure that you are well rewarded!" Elliot's voice echoed in the tunnel.

The rats stood frozen on top of one another, and then, all of a sudden, they burst out laughing. Their acrobatic formation began to sway back and forth. Having lost their balance, the three toppled into the water with a loud splash. They disappeared for a few moments, then, one by one, their heads bobbed back up. Still laughing and spitting water, the twins performed a little jig before the boy.

"I don't understand." Elliot was getting angry now with their antics. "Did I say something funny?"

"A reward! From DuBereux!" Albin was trying to catch his breath.

"The funniest thing I've heard in ages," howled Arkadi, clutching his tummy.

"Sorry, lad," Albin said, "but we don't accept money from criminals!"

"Don't deliver children to them either," Andoni added.

"Criminals!" Elliot was furious. "How dare you say that, you bunch of crazy rodents! You're the ones that kidnap children, not the Librarian!"

"Hey! No name calling, now!" Arkadi appeared genuinely hurt.

"We're just sewer maintenance, lad, that's all. Now hop on," Albin said as he climbed on top of Andoni and Arkadi.

"Yeah, hurry up. My legs are getting tired," shouted Andoni, who was at the bottom, bearing the weight of the other two.

"No!" Elliot clenched his fists. "I'm not going anywhere!"

"How' bout if I tell you that you're as important a guest down here, as you think you are up there," Albin said.

"You can't force me to go!"

"Look kid, no one's forcing you," Albin continued. "You simply have no other choice. The only way out of here is through the end of this tunnel."

"Unless you like it down here so much," Andoni added with a wink, "that you want to stay a while. . . all alone, of course."

"We have other jobs to do, y' know," Arkadi cut in.

The rats all nodded their heads in agreement. Elliot stared at them, weighing his options. Fighting was out of question. His instinct was to make a run for it. But how far could he get before he was caught? This was their turf. And even if he managed to escape, how would he find his way out of the sewers? The rats were right. He had to go along with their plan.

"C'mon, hurry up," Albin urged. "No harm will come to you. I give you my word as a chief sewer rat!"

Elliot started to climb, but the rats' rubber suits were so wet, he slipped and fell a few times. Finally, he managed to clamber up and stood wobbling on Albin's shoulders.

"What now?" he asked.

"Just sit yourself on the bike," replied Albin, giving the boy a leg up onto the seat.

"Then pedal, so you get the dynamo going and your headlights working."

Albin gave the vehicle a shove, and Elliot pushed on the pedals. The rusty mechanism let out a loud creak and lurched forward a few inches. Elliot put all his weight on the pedals, and the machine slowly started to move, flakes of rust falling off its frame. The headlights flickered and came to life. Elliot looked down over his shoulder. The rats were waving him on.

"Go, go. There's no time! Go to the end of the tunnel!"

Elliot turned and pedaled harder. The vehicle slid along the rail faster and faster. Soon he'd left the rats far behind, and he was alone in the tunnel. He pedaled and pedaled. The bike's pale yellow lights bounced off the rusty, wet walls. The tunnel twisted and turned, and it seemed to go on forever. Finally, exhausted, Elliot stopped. The bike's lights dimmed and went out completely. He sat in the dark, desperation creeping into his heart, when he saw a glimmer of light ahead. It was so faint it was almost invisible, but it was definitely there. Elliot stepped on the pedals again. Soon he could clearly see an orange glow ahead. The light grew brighter and closer. And, sure enough, before long the tunnel ended abruptly at the mouth of an enormous underground cave.

Elliot stopped and stared in amazement at a city of tents. Hundreds of makeshift shelters —large and small, tattered and torn— stood bathed in bright, warm light. The place was buzzing with life. Clusters of people and creatures were all engaged in different activities, some setting up new tents, others digging trenches or carrying food and water. Elliot didn't have a chance to admire the view for long. A hand grabbed his leg and pulled him off the vehicle. He dropped on the ground, and when he looked up, he was staring at a crossbow, which was pointed in his face.

"Before I put an arrow through your head, tell me how you got here, you little spy!" The voice belonged to a stocky man dressed in a battered, old leather coat, his belt heavy with grenades. The man was surrounded by a group of warriors covered in shiny armor. They pointed their weapons at Elliot, too.

They all looked oddly familiar. It took a second for him to realize why. They were the four who had first appeared in his bedroom. The ones who would have killed him, if the Librarian's men had not come to his rescue. Defiers! thought Elliot, instantly losing all hope. I'm dead! He closed his eyes, waiting for the worst.

"Hold it, Maddock!"

Elliot opened his eyes. A fierce-looking woman pushed through the soldiers.

"That's the child we've been looking for! Stand back at once!" she ordered.

"Well...we can never be too sure, can we?" said the man, stepping aside. "He could've been one of Morana's little spies!" Reluctantly, he lowered his crossbow, and his men lowered their weapons, too.

Maddock

"I apologize for the rude welcome," the woman said, helping Elliot to his feet. "But we have to be careful. We get attacked all the time, although we constantly keep moving our camp. My name is Runa, and I command the Defiers. Maddock, here, is my right hand man."

"You are the Leader?" Elliot was stunned. "I thought they captured you!"

"That's true, I was captured. It was the best way to divert DuBereux's attention and get you down here. I allowed myself to be caught on purpose." Her voice had a steely edge to it. "Then I disappeared down a manhole, right under Morana's nose," she added, smiling for the first time.

Elliot continued to eye her suspiciously. Like Maddock, she was dressed in leather breeches and boots. A big gun holster hung on her hip. Then he noticed the snake. It was coiled up on top of her head, peeking through her dreadlocked hair. Instinctively, Elliot took a step back.

"Don't be scared," said Runa, still smiling. "She's my best friend and my strongest weapon. She won't attack one of our friends, and I believe you are a friend, aren't you, Elliot Bade?"

Elliot didn't answer; he couldn't.

"Look," said Runa, "I know you are afraid of us. I'm sure DuBereux's told you many things about the Defiers, but none of them are true. We're not what he says we are! Far from it! He's the one seeking to destroy our beloved Great Nidor. You've seen the city, Elliot. Did it look like a happy place to you?"

Elliot hesitated. "No, it didn't," he replied. "But the Librarian's going to make it all better when he opens the Wing of the Future!"

Runa laughed coldly. "Yes, of course he will! He'd tell you anything, just so he can get his way." She paused for a moment, studying Elliot's face. "I bet he told you the story about his son."

"Yes," Elliot said. "He could have saved him, if only he'd been able to see into the Future."

Runa shook her head in disgust. "DuBereux never had a son! He has no children."

"Why would he lie about something like that?" Elliot exclaimed.

"He lied so that you'd feel sorry for him and truly wish to open the door to the Future. He had to make you believe. That was the only way the key could be released from the rock."

Elliot thought for a moment. "But I do believe! And I do want to go through that door!" he cried. "Please, I have to go back there!"

Runa narrowed her eyes as she scrutinized him. "What else did DuBereux tell you?" she asked.

Elliot stood silent.

"What else did he tell you?"

"That he'd help me save my mother," half-whispered Elliot. Runa's face filled with pity. She stepped forward and gently embraced him.

"It's all one big lie. No matter what he promised you, he never intended to let you see the Future. He wants it all for himself. You are disposable. All he needs from you is the key and your innocence."

"No! You're the one who's lying!" cried Elliot and shook her hands off him. DuBereux's words of warning about the Defiers rung in his ears. Shameless liars, who would do and say anything! Elliot knew he couldn't trust this woman. She was just trying to confuse him.

"I know what you are up to!" He fought back his angry tears. "You want the key for yourselves."

"We most certainly do!" Runa snapped. "But taking it from you, now that it is no longer in the rock, will be quite a task, I see."

"I won't give it to you," Elliot hissed. "You'll have to kill me first!"

"Elliot, I see that it's difficult for you to accept the truth. Perhaps if I tell you a story, the real story of Great Nidor, it'll change your mind."

"It won't change anything," he said, trying to sound defiant.

"Well, don't you at least want to hear it, so you can decide for yourself?"

Elliot was quiet for a moment. There was so much insistance in Runa's voice he knew he had no choice but to listen. Reluctantly, he nodded.

Runa took his hand and walked towards the first line of tents, followed by Maddock and his men.

"Great Nidor," the woman began, "was once a happy place, vibrant and full of life. Everyone was free to levitate whenever they wanted to. There were no restrictions, no spying, and no guards on every corner. The previous Librarian, Adelmar Baldric, understood the power of knowledge. He encouraged people, especially the children, to read. But like his predecessors, he also fiercely guarded the Wing of the Future." Runa paused and gazed at Elliot.

"You see, Elliot, the third door of the Library of Time was never meant to be opened. Ever! And for a very good reason, too. The Future is sacred knowledge, and as tempting as it may be, it must not be revealed. Above all, it must not be changed."

"Why?" asked Elliot.

"Anyone who tampers with the Future can set off a chain of events so catastrophic that they, in the end, could destroy our whole Universe," explained Runa. "The past Librarians of Great Nidor have always had enough wisdom to understand this terrible danger and have used their power to guard the Future. They kept its door closed, passing the key from one generation to the next.

"And then Magnus DuBereux came along. He refused to believe in the perils of tampering with the Future. He was on a mission to control Time: to reshape our Future, twist our Present, and destroy our Past. Back then, when he was a member of the Chancellor's Council, he started to gain support among the Chancellors and challenged Adelmar Baldric to do what no one had ever dared to do. Open the Future! Baldric feared that his Librarianship was under threat, and he decided to hide the key. Indeed, it was a lucky thing he did. Just as Baldric had feared, DuBereux, with the support of the Chancellor's Council, betrayed him.

"DuBereux took Baldric's place and arrested Baldric's daughter, Teah. They put great pressure on the poor child to tell the new Council where the key was. But it was so well-hidden even she didn't know how to find it. She was never seen or heard from again. We mourn the loss of her life, just as we do her father's. She would have been a true Librarian of Time." Runa's voice trailed off as she tried to compose herself.

"DuBereux's been on a quest to find the key from the moment he stole the Librarianship," she continued, "and finally, he succeeded. He found you and the key before we could stop him!"

Runa fell silent.

"Did DuBereux kill Baldric?" asked Elliot.

"He did. Baldric knew what his fate would be and perhaps the fate of his daughter, too. He made the ultimate sacrifice, Elliot! He knew the importance of protecting the Future. Few are able to do such a brave thing."

"And what are you going to do with me?"

"We shall retrieve the key that you hold. Then you will be sent home."

"And I won't get to see the Future, go inside, and… help my mom?" Elliot's voice trembled, for he already sensed what the answer would be.

"No, Elliot," answered Runa. "We never make promises we cannot keep."

• ◯ •

Runa, Elliot, and Maddock finally reached the heart of the tent city. There was a warm, inviting glow all around them. Elliot saw its inhabitants busily going about their daily chores. The sounds and smells of the place reminded him of home. Then he noticed the children. High above the tents, they were somersaulting, doing back flips, and playing tag. The cave echoed with their carefree laughter.

"Look! They're levitating!" Elliot exclaimed, stopping in his tracks. He turned to Runa. "So, this is where all the kids are." Elliot suddenly remembered Vergil's words. "It's true then! You do kidnap children!" he cried and looked at Runa accusingly.

"Yes, we do," she admitted. "But we prefer to call it saving children. Saving them from the miserable life they have up there, permanently locked indoors, without books, without knowledge."

Runa was interrupted by the shrill ringing of a bell. The kids in the air scrambled and glided down to the ground. The noisy group then disappeared into a large, hangar-like tent. Soon, Elliot saw more children arrive in little flocks. They filed past him.

"Let me show you their school," said Runa. "It's where our old and wise Scholars relate their stories and pass them on to the young."

Runa ushered Elliot towards the canopied entrance. Maddock followed them. Just as they were about to step inside, Runa drew Elliot close and whispered, "You shall also meet Theodor, the real Leader of the Defiers!"

Inside, the school looked even bigger. Strings of lanterns dangled from wooden beams, illuminating three rows of long tables set up in the middle of the tent. Behind each table sat dozens of elderly, white-haired men and women. The Scholars at the first table were busy scribbling with their quills

on pieces of dried parchment. Once they had finished their pages, they passed them on to the next table. There, the second group of Scholars bound the leaves together and turned them into crude books. They carried the completed manuscripts over to the third table and handed them to the last set of Scholars, who, in turn, read aloud from these tomes to the children gathered before them. Every once in a while, the young pupils would repeat something they had heard, then fall silent and continue to listen. There was something magical in their chorus of words, and Elliot had the sudden urge to join in.

With a shake of her head, Runa held him back. She quietly led him to a Scholar who sat apart from the rest. The man had a prominant nose and a thick, silvery-gray beard.

"Theodor," Runa addressed him with great reverence. "This is Elliot Bade."

The Scholar looked up from his book and stared at Elliot for a long moment. "Where is the rock?" Theodor asked softly.

"Unfortunately," Runa said in a hushed voice, "DuBereux managed to get the boy to the Clocksmyth."

"Aagh!" Theodor exclaimed, his face growing very pale.

"They took a Stingray straight to the workshop. We couldn't intercept them."

"Let me see the key," Theodor whispered and placed a large magnifying glass over his right eye. Elliot extended his hand. Theodor grasped it, held it close, and carefully studied the boy's palm.

"Just as I feared!" he said, with a look of dismay. "Runa, there is a timer in the key! If the door to the Future is not opened, the key will self-destruct and kill its bearer."

"What?" Elliot gasped in horror, snatching back his hand.

The old Scholar shook his head grimly. "Unfortunately, no one can remove it now, not even the Clocksmyth who put it there. This boy shall have to open the door to the Future."

"But how much time do I have?" asked Elliot, his heart pounding. "What if it goes off before I get to the door?"

"Time is relative," Theodore replied. "Above ground, it flows differently than it does down here. It has only been a blink of an eye since you disappeared into the manhole. Yet to you it feels like it has been much, much

longer." The Scholar produced a pocket watch from the tool belt strapped around his waist. "By my estimation, you have but a Moon-dial and three-quarts left. That is an hour, by your Earthly measures."

Suddenly, Maddock brought his fist down on the table with a loud bang. "I say we keep him with us. Let the key destroy itself. So what if the boy dies?" he thundered. "At least DuBereux won't get his hands on the Future."

A hush fell over all the long tables. Slowly, Theodor rose up from his bench.

"Shame on you!" he bellowed. "First of all, a child's life is sacred. If we commit such a crime, we shall be no better than DuBereux and his evil followers. As for the key, come what may, it must continue to exist. Adelmar Baldric could have destroyed it himself, but he did not!"

"Are you saying we must give up all that we've fought for?" Maddock cried.

"I am sorry," Theodor said with great bitterness, "but there is no other way! DuBereux has outsmarted us." He turned to Runa. "You had better take the boy back up there, before it is too late."

"Wait!" came a hurried voice from the tent's entrance. "There is a way out, yes, yes!"

Elliot spun around and froze. He couldn't believe his eyes.

It was Vergil!

Stunned, Elliot looked at Theodor, then at Runa.

"But he…he is one of them! What's he doing here?"

"Actually, Elliot," Runa said reassuringly, "he's one of us! He serves DuBereux, but he is our eyes and ears in the Council."

"What do you suggest, Vergil?" asked Theodor.

"There's one person, see, who can stop the timer and save the key," said Vergil, as he leapt on the table in front of them. "Teah Baldric! Adelmar's daughter, yes, yes."

"Vergil, have you lost your mind?" gasped Runa.

" 'Course not, no!"

"But, she's dead!"

"She's not, oh no! 'Tis what DuBereux's led us to believe, see."

"Are you sure?" asked Theodor, shaking his head in disbelief.

"Saw her with my own two eyes, yes, yes. Up on them screens, you see," Vergil replied, then turned to Elliot. "Remember, yes? The Wing of the Present, you were there!"

Elliot hesitated. "I did see a girl," he finally told them, "with blue eyes."

"Where is she? Where has DuBereux kept her all this time?" Runa could hardly contain her excitement.

"Locked up, you see, yes! In a secret dungeon. Right under the Library, yes."

"What difference does it make if she's still alive?" Maddock growled.

"The boy, he has to pass the key to her, you see," Vergil answered, then added, " 'Tis dangerous, but worth a try, yes?"

Everyone stared at the creature in shock.

"Vergil's right!" Runa turned to look at Elliot. "If you pass the key to her, Teah automatically becomes the new Librarian," she cried. "The Future will be safe!"

"Elliot, would you do that?" Vergil asked urgently. "Pass the key to Teah, yes?"

"No! That is an unacceptable proposition," interrupted Theodor. "The passing of the key is the most perilous of rituals with tragic consequences should it fail to work. Not only do we stand to lose the key forever, but both children could die!"

" 'Tis worth a try, see. Them kids are stronger than we think, yes, yes!"

Elliot felt a dull ache in the palm of his hand where the key was embedded. He saw himself standing before the door to the Future. He could hear DuBereux's words, the promises he had made, and all the wonderful possibilities that awaited him.

"Enough!" Theodor snapped. "It is not a question of their strength, but of their true willingness to perform such a task. I know that this boy here is not ready to part with the key. I can sense it in his heart! He must go back before it is too late."

"Very well then. He must go back and open the door," said Runa, her eyes flashing. "But DuBereux won't lay his hands on the Future without a fight!"

Theodor solemnly nodded. "Call all men to arms!" he ordered, and Runa immediately began to uncoil the snake from her hair.

"And Teah?" asked Vergil. "Her life may not be spared, see, once the Future is unlocked, oh no."

"We shall attempt to rescue her first, before we strike," replied Theodor.

"So, I take the boy back up to DuBereux, yes?" Vergil's voice was now full of resignation.

"Those are my orders!" the Scholar replied gravely.

Runa turned to Elliot with a look of deep hurt and regret. "Soon after you open the door, you shall witness a bloody battle. If we allow DuBereux to start changing the Future, it will mean the end of us all."

Elliot cast his eyes over the tables covered in parchment and crudely-bound books. He could see fear in the faces of the children, and his stomach turned.

"Come, Elliot, time for you to go," Theodor said.

Runa, Maddock, and Elliot left the school followed by Vergil and Theodor. Tethered to a pole, a creature similar to a sea lion floated in the air, waiting for them. It had a large leather saddle strapped on its back.

"She flies us back to the manhole, see," Vergil said, taking the reins.

"And the ambush by the river?" asked Elliot. "Won't DuBereux suspect something's up?"

"Them guards are where we left' em, see."

"And they won't realize we've been gone all this time?"

Theodor stopped and looked at his pocket watch. "They will still be at the very first stages of fighting our men when you return. You shall arrive safely at the Library within the key's allotted time."

Vergil hopped on the sea lion's back and motioned Elliot to follow him. The boy hesitated for a moment, then gingerly straddled his new ride.

"Good-bye, Elliot," said Runa. "Look after yourself and remember what I told you about DuBereux."

"Bye!" Elliot murmured and tried to smile. "I'm sorry," he added, surprised at his own words.

But Runa did not hear his apology because the strange sea lion was already in the air and rising fast.

From high above, Elliot watched as men and women began to run out of their shabby tents, weapons in their hands.

They're getting ready to go to war! he thought.

He felt in some way guilty. His palm tingled, and he tried to imagine what whould happen next. The door to the Future was waiting for him, and he was

86

going to open it. But at what cost? And to what end? These questions had entered his heart, and confused, Elliot yearned for simple answers.

• ☾ •

Elliot was still troubled as they rose above the ground. They emerged through an open shaft, right beside the Library of Time.

"Vergil, we're in the wrong place!" he whispered. "Where's the manhole? Where are we?"

"We'll get to the manhole, you see," said Vergil. "But not before I show you something, oh no!"

After quickly dismounting the sea lion and deftly avoiding the Library's Sentries, the pair stood in the long shadow of the Wing of the Past, their backs pressed against its stone wall.

"Trap door, see." Vergil pointed to a very faint outline of a square under their feet. The creature motioned to Elliot to step aside.

The door slid open to reveal a steep stairway going straight down into a fathomless pit.

"Where are you taking me?" Elliot asked.

"You'll find out soon, yes, yes," replied Vergil.

A few bare light bulbs showed them the way to the bottom. Elliot followed Vergil through a warren of narrow passageways. The number of bulbs gradually decreased until there were none, and it was pitch black.

"Vergil, I can't see a thing," Elliot whispered, desperately searching for a wall to touch for support.

"Then use your ears to follow me, yes."

Vergil started to creep forward again. Elliot crept behind him, listening to the sound of the creature's claws scratching on the stone floor. The stale air was suffocating, and he removed his hot robe. After a long, tedious, dark journey, finally they stopped. Scant light filtered down from a vent somewhere high above their heads. Elliot strained his eyes and realized they were standing next to a caged door.

Vergil tapped on its heavy iron bars several times. For a few long moments, nothing happened. Then, from somewhere deep inside the cell, came the

sound of rattling chains. Elliot dropped his robe and gasped. Out of the darkness, like a ghost, a thin, pale girl appeared. Her hair was long and unkempt, her clothes grimy and tattered.

"Vergil, is that you?" the girl whispered as she slowly shuffled towards them.

" 'Tis me, yes, yes. I bring the boy."

With great effort, the girl got close to the cell door. She stared directly at Elliot with haunting blue eyes.

I know who this is! he thought and held his breath.

"Hello, Elliot. I'm Teah Baldric. I'm very pleased to meet you," she said with the most bewitching smile. There was a lilt to her voice, and like music, it rose and fell over their heads.

Elliot felt himself blush, and for the first time, he was thankful for the darkness.

She took another step towards them, then winced in pain and stopped.

He looked down and, to his horror, saw that her bare feet were shackled in a contraption studded with iron thorns. Attached to this monstrosity was a heavy chain, which Teah had dragged to its full length.

"Are you going to help us?" she asked with another smile.

"He still believes in DuBereux, see," Vergil said. "The wicked man has promised him things, yes, yes."

Teah frowned, then nodded.

"Elliot," she began slowly, choosing her words carefully, "I know how hard it must be for you to decide what to do. I know about loss, believe me! About desperately wanting to help someone you love, wanting to save their life, and then having to make a choice."

"You mean your father, don't you?" said Elliot. He remembered the story of Adelmar Baldric.

"Yes, I could have saved him. I could have told DuBereux where my father had hidden the key."

"But you didn't?"

"No, and although I have regrets, I'm sure I did exactly what he wanted me to do," Teah said.

Elliot watched as a single tear glistened in the corner of her eye, then rolled down her pale cheek.

She brushed it away with her hand.

"DuBereux wouldn't have spared my father's life anyway, even if I had told him everything," she said. "He is a cruel, cruel man. I doubt he'll spare yours either, once you open the door to the Future."

Elliot looked into her sad blue eyes. A feeling of a deep and profound connection to Teah suddenly overwhelmed him. If he had any doubts as to what he was about to say, they were now gone.

"I want to help!"

"Are you sure?"

"Yes, I'm positive," said Elliot. "I know what my mother would want me to do!"

"You are willing to pass the key to me?"

"I am."

"You have to understand that if we succeed, the Future will remain unchanged, and what will be, will be."

"Just tell me what I need to do."

"You have to hold her hand, see, see," said Vergil, barely containing his excitement.

"Yes, and not let go until the key is in mine." Teah's face was very grave. "And I really mean do not let go, no matter what, no matter how much pain you feel. If one of us lets go before the key has changed hands, we'll both…"

"Die! Die, yes, yes!" Vergil finished her words hurriedly. "But brave children think not of dying, oh no. You'll do just fine, see, see!"

Teah glanced at him and then back at Elliot.

"Are you ready, Elliot?" Teah asked.

"I am."

Vergil stepped between them. "Right then, yes! On my count… One…"

Teah pushed her right hand through the iron bars.

"Two…"

Elliot extended his.

"Three!"

They grabbed hands and held tight.

Elliot closed his eyes.

At first, nothing happened. Then came a low rumble, which grew louder and louder. The floor began to tremble. The heavy iron bars began to vibrate. One by one, the bolts that held them together flew off. With a deafening crash, the prison cage shattered and then collapsed around them. The heavy shackles around Teah's ankles snapped open, releasing her feet.

A strong gust of wind lifted them off the shaking ground. It spun them around like rag dolls. Round and round they flew, faster and faster. The vortex was so strong, Elliot was sure his arm would be ripped off.

He almost let go of Teah's hand. Teah almost let go of his. But they both hung on.

Elliot felt objects hitting his body. He didn't know what they were, but he was too scared to open his eyes. Then, all of a sudden, the wind stopped.

They floated in empty space and in complete silence. It was dead calm. Nothing moved.

Maybe it's over, Elliot thought. But Teah was still gripping his hand. He waited.

The room grew hot. Oven hot! Their skin quickly erupted in blisters. The pain was unbearable, but just when Elliot thought he couldn't hold on any longer, the heat abated.

He felt raindrops on his parched skin. It was such a relief to have the cool rain falling on his overheated body. He relaxed a bit. But then the rain intensified, and it grew very, very cold.

Elliot began to shiver; his teeth chattered. A ferocious hailstorm was upon them now, lashing at their faces.

"I can't hold on any longer!" he cried out in pain.

"Elliot, don't let go!" Teah yelled back.

But the tempest's fury was stronger than his will. He began to lose his grip. His fingers were being pried open one by one.

No! thought Elliot. We are not going to die! We are not going to die! he repeated over and over as he desperately clung to Teah.

Just as he felt her hand begin to slip away, the storm suddenly subsided. The two fell to the floor, wet and exhausted, but still holding onto each other.

They lay there for a few moments, trying to catch their breath. Finally, slowly, they opened their eyes.

"It's over, Elliot," Teah gasped.

"Brave, brave children! Well done, yes, yes!" Vergil rushed over to them. "Now, we have to get you out of here!"

Elliot looked at his hand. The key was gone, except for a faint red mark where it used to be. He looked back at Teah. She was holding her hand up for him to see.

The key was there, buried right in the middle of her palm.

"We did it!" she said.

She smiled, then turned to the creature. "What's the plan Vergil?"

"A sea lion will take you to the Defiers, yes. They're readying themselves for an attack on the Library, you see."

"And what about you two?" Teah asked.

"We return to the Wing of the Future, see."

"But that's too dangerous!" she cried. "Come with me!"

Vergil shook his head. "DuBereux will be waiting for the boy to open the door, see. He must not suspect anything has gone amiss, no!"

Teah frowned as she thought about Vergil's plan. "A surprise strike on the Library would be best," she began slowly. "DuBereux won't have the time to organize a defense. His army does outnumber ours, but if it's not pre-pared, we stand a much better chance of winning." She turned to Elliot with a look of concern on her face. "Will you be alright?"

"Don't worry about me," Elliot bravely said, putting back on his robe. "Just make sure you're not too late!"

Teah reached out and squeezed Elliot's hand. "Then it's decided. Let's go!"

With Vergil leading the way, the three began to make their way back through the dungeon's dark maze of tunnels.

"I wish we could see in here," said Elliot with frustration.

Suddenly, a strong white beam shot out and lit up the passageway. Behind him stood Teah, her palm shining like a torch, so bright that it nearly blinded him.

"Wow!" he exclaimed.

"The key knows it's in the hands of a true Librarian," Teah said as she hurried ahead.

Sea Lion

Elliot, impressed, followed her and Vergil out of the dungeon.

Soon, the three were back at the secret shaft where the sea lion was waiting. "We all share the ride for part of the way, yes," whispered Vergil. "Me and him must slip back to them guards, you see."

The two children sat in the saddle one behind the other, Teah's arms around Elliot's waist. The sea lion dove into the tunnel and swiftly transported them to the manhole through which Elliot had originally fallen.

"From here Teah goes alone, yes," Vergil instructed and nudged Elliot.

The sea lion had maneuvered itself so that Vergil and Elliot could easily clamber back out.

Elliot cautiously stuck his head above ground and realized that the guards were indeed right where he had left them. They stood in a tight circle around the manhole, their backs to him. With shields held over their heads, they were deflecting the fierce rain of incoming arrows.

"See you soon," Teah said as she took over the reins. Elliot pulled himself up onto the cobbled harbor street. Then, still kneeling by the manhole, he watched as Teah sank back down into the darkness. A piercing whistle startled him, and he jumped to his feet. Just as suddenly as the attack had started, it was over. The arrows stopped falling, and with a look of relief on their faces, the guards lowered their shields.

"To the Library of Time, yes!" barked Vergil, and before Elliot knew it, they were marching once again.

They entered the building through the main gate and crossed over the drawbridge to the Wing of the Future. On the other side they came upon a chilling scene. All the Chancellors, trembling with fear, were standing in a line before DuBereux. The Librarian was pacing back and forth, his face full of rage. Suddenly, he stopped in front of Chancellor Morana. Her posture was no longer upright and menacing. Cowering, she stared at her feet.

"And for this to happen today, of all days!" he shouted. "To have the Leader of the Defiers in your grasp and then allow your quarry to escape. What say you, woman?" he asked, as he began to pace up and down again.

"Sir," began Morana in a faltering voice, "I had it under control, I swear. My men had the Leader cornered... And just before your Librarianship arrived ... I don't know how it happened ... she vanished."

"Do you take me for a fool?!" DuBereux roared. "Under control you say? I think not! Your incompetence is treason of the highest order." He shook his head in disgust. "I think, Morana, I must find a replacement for you." The rest of the Chancellors nodded in agreement, relieved that they were not on the receiving end of the Librarian's wrath.

"I shall have you..." The Librarian suddenly stopped in mid-sentence. And, almost as if he had eyes on the back of his head, DuBereux turned on his heels. His face transformed in an instant. "Elliot! My dear boy, here you are!" The Librarian rushed towards Elliot, arms outstretched, and grabbed both his hands. Elliot's heart almost stopped. Fortunately, DuBereux did not look for the key, but led him straight to the door. "I trust our city was to your liking? I trust Vergil was an excellent guide?"

"Yes, very." Elliot nodded vigorously, trying to stay calm.

"Gentlemen, pray gather around. It's the moment we have all been waiting for. We shall take a look into the Future!"

The Chancellors quickly formed a semi-circle around the door. Morana was last to join them.

"You!" barked DuBereux, pointing a crooked finger at her. "You, madam, have lost the privilege to witness a moment as great as this! I relieve you from your duties and place you under arrest!"

Morana dropped to her knees, her hands clasped in front of her. "Sir...Your Librarianship, please!" she wailed.

DuBereux did not look at her. "Take her away!" he commanded.

Morana collapsed onto the ground, tears streaming down her bony face. Two guards grabbed her under the arms and pulled her up. She struggled, showing amazing strength for her skinny frame, as the burly guards dragged her away.

"Wait!" the Librarian stopped them. "Take her down to my secret dungeon and bring Teah Baldric up here."

There was a loud gasp from the group of Chancellors.

"Teah Baldric!" all of them exclaimed in one voice.

"Yes, yes. You heard right. Teah Baldric! That obstinate creature has to witness this. I suspect she may rather enjoy the grand opening!" DuBereux looked extremely pleased with himself.

Elliot froze. He glanced at Vergil. He could tell the creature looked worried.

"Err… Master. We don't have time for that, no, no. The timer on the key, you see…"

"Ah, yes," DuBereux frowned. "As always, Vergil, you are most prudent. The girl can wait. Let us proceed, Elliot. Come here, my child!" DuBereux's frown changed to a radiant smile.

Elliot saw Vergil shake his head in warning as he stepped over to the door. Where were Teah and the Defiers? he thought frantically. He had to stall DuBereux just a little longer. "Sir, I'd like to make a wish." Elliot tried to keep his voice even.

"Anything, my dear friend," said the Librarian, beaming.

"I wish to know about my mother and the Colonel," said Elliot. He held his breath.

"What makes you think I am privy to such information?"

"You are the Librarian, sir. You may have read something about them in one of those books I saw in the Wing of the Past," Elliot replied.

"Perchance, I do believe I have," said DuBereux, drawing the boy nearer to him.

"Once upon a time," he began softly in a hypnotizing voice, "a man called the Colonel found himself a widower with a small child on his hands. But the powers above had ordained for him a brilliant career, that of an astronaut, a sailor to the stars. He chose to dedicate his life to his celestial travels and not his little daughter, you see. One day, he discovered her playing with his precious books and instruments. Alas, the naughty girl had done something much worse! She had taken his Moon Rock out of its special box. Outraged, the Colonel severely punished his daughter, and soon after he had her sent away.

"She was schooled far from home, brought up by total strangers. With every passing year, the girl saw less and less of her distant father. Naturally, she grew to despise both the man and his work. And so it came to be that the girl became a young woman who vowed never to speak to or see her father again." The Librarian finished the story with a twinkle in his eyes. "Now, fancy this, my little friend!" DuBereux chuckled. "If the Colonel had not intervened, that girl would have stood where you are standing today!"

Elliot looked puzzled. "I'm not sure I understand, sir."

"We would have found the key much sooner, my dear child. The little girl, your mother, could have been our key bearer, not you. If only the Colonel had allowed her to hold that Moon Rock but a little longer," DuBereux explained in a wistful voice. "Now, without any further ado, pray place your precious palm in the lock," he ordered.

Elliot had no time to think about what he had just heard. He looked back at Vergil, who now gave him a nod of encouragement. Elliot turned to face the door, his heart pounding loudly in his chest. Sweat trickled down his back as he slowly lifted his trembling hand and placed it in the lock mechanism. There was dead silence. No one moved, except for Chancellor Cadogan, who clapped his hands a little too soon. DuBereux shot him a deadly glance, and the poor man froze on the spot. Everybody's eyes were on Elliot. Nothing happened. Elliot looked at the Librarian. The smile on DuBereux's face quickly disappeared.

"What?"

"Maybe I can try again," said Elliot, quickly pulling his hand out. "Maybe I didn't do it right!"

DuBereux was beginning to look frustrated.

"Yes, yes! Of course. Try again. Hurry up!"

Elliot placed his hand in the lock one more time, dreading what was going to happen next. A few long moments passed.

"This is not possible!" cried DuBereux. "What are you doing, boy? Let me see!" He rushed to Elliot and grabbed his hand. His eyes widened. "Where is the key? What have you done, you fool?"

Elliot tried to pull his hand free, but the Librarian's grip was as strong as a pair of pliers.

"I had the key, I swear," stammered Elliot. "It was here, in my palm, just a minute ago!"

DuBereux's face distorted with anger. He bared his crooked teeth. "Lie not to me, boy! Where is it?"

"I don't know, sir."

"You do know!" DuBereux shook Elliot violently. "You betrayed me! You miserable, little traitor! I shall kill you myself!" He lifted his hand to strike

Elliot, but at that very moment, as fast as a bullet, Vergil sprang through the air and sank his teeth and claws into the Librarian's arm.

Blinded by rage, DuBereux shook the creature off. Vergil hit the wall and fell to the floor. A second later, Vergil was back on top of the Librarian, scratching and biting again. The Librarian cried in pain and finally let go of Elliot.

Elliot scrambled back a few steps and watched in horror as a guard struck Vergil with his spear. Poor Vergil flew over their heads. Elliot gasped and started to inch his way towards the drawbridge.

"The boy! Get the boy!" shouted DuBereux.

His shouts were cut short by the great roar of a war cry coming from beyond the Library's walls. One of the Chancellors ran to the balustrades, then turned back in terror. "We're under attack! It's the Defiers! There are hundreds of them!"

The Chancellors panicked. Despite DuBereux's shouts to stay together, they ran in different directions. Elliot could hear gunshots and other explosions. He had lost sight of Vergil in all the commotion. Was he dead? Then, out of nowhere, a powerful blow struck the side of his head. His legs buckled, and as he fell, he looked up.

DuBereux towered over him, dagger in hand, poised to strike.

· ◐ ·

Elliot could feel something cool press against his forehead. Slowly he came to and opened his eyes. The blurred image of a face floated in front of him.

DuBereux! he thought in terror. Then the face came into focus. It was Teah! She was kneeling next to him, gently dabbing his forehead with a wet cloth. "Hi, Elliot," she said with a smile. "Good to see you again."

Elliot lifted his head to get a better look at her. She was wearing a breast-plate of armor on top of her tattered robe. Although covered in soot, her smile was just as beautiful as he remembered it. "Am I dreaming again?" he whispered.

She laughed. "No, Elliot, you're not dreaming. We won! It's over!"

"Where's DuBereux? I thought he was going to kill me!"

"He managed to escape. But we'll find him soon." Elliot heard a familiar voice and looked up. Runa was standing above him. Behind her was Maddock, holding his crossbow. Both looked tired, dirty, and bruised.

"And what about Vergil? What happened to him? He saved my life!" Elliot cried as Runa helped him to his feet.

"I'm here my friend, yes," the creature called out, his scaly body wrapped in bandages. "Takes more than that, you see, to get rid of old Vergil," he added, as he limped over to Elliot. "Care to have a look out there, yes? See what your bravery did achieve, yes?"

Still feeling dizzy, Elliot walked over to the balustrade and looked down. The signs of a great battle stretched out before him. He could see smoldering buildings and rubble where once walls had stood. Even the statue of the Librarian lay broken in pieces on the ground. From all corners of the square, the people of Great Nidor were coming out in droves, and some had already begun to levitate with joy. Up in the sky, hundreds of whales were flocking together to witness the city's jubilation and to celebrate it with their songs.

Teah stepped beside him.

"We have a lot of work to do now," she said. "This will once again be a happy place. Thanks to you, Elliot."

"Well, I didn't do much, did I?" he said sheepishly. "I blacked out at the most important moment!"

"You did more than enough. You gave us back the key."

"What are you going to do with it now?"

"Just as my father did, I shall try to keep the key away from the hands of the likes of Magnus DuBereux. That evil man is gone now, but sooner or later, someone else will try to open the door of the Future. It's my duty to protect it." She looked into Elliot's eyes for a long moment. "And now, I'm afraid, it's time for you to leave."

"Leave?"

Teah placed her arms on his shoulders. "Elliot, you belong to a different world! Have you forgotten?"

"No, I haven't. But I was hoping I could stay a little bit longer."

"I'm sorry, you can't," she said, then added, "but, who knows, you might visit us again some day."

Elliot took a long look at the amazing city. There was still so much he wanted to see. "Well, I guess it's time to say good-bye then," he whispered.

Elliot turned to Runa, Maddock, and Vergil. Runa embraced him, and he noticed that the snake in her hair was gone. Seeing the question in his eyes, she said, "Sadly, we lost her in the battle."

"You're a brave young man, Elliot," Maddock said. His voice was filled with respect. He was about to shake Elliot's hand, but then changed his mind. Instead, he gave Elliot a clumsy bear hug. Everybody laughed.

Vergil had no strength to jump in Elliot's arms, so Elliot gently picked him up.

"Been wanting to say sorry, yes. For having scared you behind that curtain, see…," Vergil began, but Elliot stopped him.

"It's okay, I forgive you," said Elliot, letting Vergil nuzzle his cheek. I hope Rupert turns out to be as nice as you, he thought, suddenly remembering the Colonel's dog. Oh, no! he thought, as something else struck him. The Moon Rock! I'm going back without it!

"Elliot, there's one in your pocket," Teah said, as if she had read his thoughts. "Don't worry. Your grandfather will never know the difference." Her blue eyes twinkled.

"Then I'm ready to go. How do I get back?"

"Well," Teah said, "let me first take your gravity bracelet off. You won't need it anymore." She held his hand and turned one of the dials of the bracelet. The bracelet snapped open and slipped off Elliot's wrist. He felt a huge weight fall away from his shoulders. He lifted up, his body as light as a feather. Startled, he kicked his feet, trying to stay on the floor. "Don't be afraid, Elliot," Teah said. "Let yourself go. It's just like swimming."

Elliot stopped struggling and allowed himself to float gently a few feet up. His fear was replaced by a feeling of sheer joy. "I'm levitating!" he shouted, looking down at Teah as he rose even higher. "Look! I can do back flips… and cartwheels!"

"Elliot, it's time," Teah called out. "Your way home's through here."

She pointed at the door to the Future.

"We wish the Past or the Present would take you back…but…we know they won't. Looks like you and the Future were meant to be…."

Elliot stared at the door. "But I thought no one was allowed in."

"This wing owes you a lot. It's a way of saying thank you." Teah smiled.

"Will I know my future? Get to change it?" asked Elliot.

"Once inside, you will indeed see what awaits you," she replied solemnly, "but the moment you find yourself back home, everything that was revealed to you will be erased from your memory!"

"So I get to see my future, and at the same time I don't." Elliot smiled wryly.

"There's something else." Teah sighed and lowered her gaze. "When you get back, you shall have no memory of what took place here in Great Nidor. You won't remember a thing."

A single tear rolled down Teah's cheek. Impulsively, Elliot reached out and gently wiped it away. Oh, I'll remember you! How can I forget? Elliot thought and fought back his own tears.

"As to whether you will get to change your future," Teah continued, "I'm afraid you cannot. You are not the Librarian of Time."

With those words, Teah walked quickly over to the door and placed her hand in the lock. The mechanism clicked, and the portal to the Future slid open with a hissing sound. Bright white light shone from inside.

Elliot hesitated. Yes, he really wanted to see what the Future had in store for him. Was his mother going to get better? Would she and his grandfather ever get along? What would happen to him? Was he ever to return to Great Nidor? But he also wanted to remember. Especially Teah.

He looked back over his shoulder at the new friends he had made. They were all standing there, waving good-bye.

"Go in, Elliot!" Teah smiled. "It's beautiful!"

"Good-bye," he called out one last time. Then he stepped inside.

Just as the door was about to close, he felt someone step next to him. A hand squeezed his, and Elliot heard a familiar voice full of music whisper in his ear, "You are not the Librarian of Time, but I am!"

And then the two children were engulfed by the white light.

It really was beautiful!

•●•

The moment Elliot opened his eyes he knew exactly what to do. Smoke was filling up his room, and it was already very difficult to breathe. He grabbed Apollo and tucked him safely under his pajama shirt. Then he ran to his mother's bedroom.

"Mom, we have to get out of the house!" he yelled, shaking her awake. "Now!" They rushed outside, barely escaping.

Much later, as they stood watching their house burn, he tried to comfort her. "We could go and stay with the Colonel," he said.

His mother's eyes widened. "You know about your grandfather!" she gasped.

Before Elliot could reply, a firefighter hurried to their side.

"Are you hurt?" the firefighter asked, handing them a couple of blankets. "You guys had a very lucky escape."

"We're fine," replied Elliot's mother. "Thank you." And she was right. Miraculously, they had made it out without a scratch, apart from the curious red mark on the palm of Elliot's right hand. Elliot's mother gently wrapped a blanket around her son's shoulders.

"Who told you about the Colonel?"

Elliot didn't answer.

How could he? There were a thousand questions buzzing in his head that he could not answer, no matter how hard he tried. What had made him wake up when he did? How did he know about the Colonel? Whose blue eyes did he kept seeing each time he closed his own? He felt as if the answers were there, somewhere in his mind, but he simply could not find them. Elliot hugged his mother and looked up at the sky. Just as he had strangely foreseen the fire, he could foresee something else. His life was about to change. He did not know how, but he was certain that incredible adventures awaited him.

A sliver of moon peeked from behind some clouds, smiled upon Elliot and his mother, and then quickly disappeared.

· ● ◗ ☽ ○ ☾ ◖ ● ·

First published in 2007 by Simply Read Books
www.simplyreadbooks.com

Text and Illustrations © 2007 Boriana and Vladimir Todorov

Book design by Elisa Gutiérrez

Cataloguing in Publication Data Available

ISBN 978-1-894965-77-4

Printed in Singapore

10 9 8 7 6 5 4 3 2 1

www.themoonrock.com